# Api and the Boy Stranger

◇ *A Village Creation Tale* ◇

PATRICIA RODDY
*pictures by* LYNNE RUSSELL

**DIAL BOOKS FOR YOUNG READERS**

*New* York

*For Matthew*
*With special thanks to Abi Adjoualé*

P. R.


*For Lucy and Marilyn, with love*

L. R.

Published by Dial Books for Young Readers
A Division of Penguin Books USA Inc.
375 Hudson Street · New York, New York 10014

Text copyright © 1994 by Patricia Roddy
Pictures copyright © 1994 by Lynne Russell
Design by Ann Finnell
All rights reserved
Printed in Hong Kong
by South China Printing Company (1988) Limited
First Edition
1 3 5 7 9 10 8 6 4 2

Library of Congress Cataloging in Publication Data
Roddy, Patricia.
Api and the boy stranger : a village creation tale
by Patricia Roddy ; illustrated by Lynne Russell.—1st ed.
p. cm.
Summary: In this Ivory Coast legend, Api and her family are repaid
for their kindness to a stranger with a mysterious warning to leave
their village and go to the other side of the river Amman.
ISBN 0-8037-1221-9 (trade).—ISBN 0-8037-1222-7 (lib. bdg.)
[1. Folklore—Côte d'Ivoire.]
I. Russell, Lynne, ill. II. Title.
PZ8.1.R64Ap 1994 398.21—dc20 [E] 93-8359 CIP AC

The paintings for this book were created by using oil pastel
on watercolor paper. The artist's interpretations for the landscapes
and homes of Api's village are based on photos from the actual
village as it exists today. Clothing patterns are based on
West African designs.

## Pronunciation Guide and Glossary

*Ahelé* ◇ ah-HEL-ay (hello)

*Akyé* ◇ ah-KEE-yay

*Amman* ◇ ah-MAHN

*Api* ◇ AH-pee

*Chiadon* ◇ SHEE-ah-dahn

*Foutou* ◇ Foo-too

(a common food found in Ivory Coast;
made by pounding boiled roots and plantain,
a type of banana, into round, doughy masses)

*Gnouen* ◇ noo-ENN

*Hen Ko* ◇ HEN ko

*Kousso* ◇ KOO-so

*N'Dé* ◇ enn-DAY

*Sawa* ◇ SAH-wah

*Va* ◇ VAH

Deep in the bush of Ivory Coast, in the land of the *Akyé*, when children refuse to share their food, mothers say, "Remember the ancestors!" Then from time to time when the moon is full, children gather around a fire to hear a tale like this one.

Early one morning, long ago, the ancestors were busy preparing a feast. It was a *Hen Ko*, a day when a baby would be named. A small girl called Api sat listening under a mango tree in the court-yard, or *sawa*.

She heard her mother pounding the foutou: Tue, ta. Tue, ta.

She heard Kousso's mother stirring a great pot of sauce: Ngub. Ngub.

And she heard Chiadon's mother grilling chicken: Pssssss. Pssssss.

"When will we eat?" she asked her mother.

"It's too early," her mother answered.

"And when will the drummers begin so that we may dance?"

"Be patient."

So Api leaned back against the tree, closed her eyes, and
listened once again:
Tue, ta. Tue, ta.
Ngub. Ngub.
Pssssss. Pssssss.
Tue, ta. Tue, ta. . . .

Suddenly the sawa was silent. Api opened her eyes. Everyone
was staring at a stranger, a very thin boy carrying a bowl.

He walked slowly toward Kousso's mother and held out his bowl.

Kousso's mother turned away and continued stirring the sauce: Ngub. Ngub.

Then the boy approached Chiadon's mother and held out his bowl again.

Chiadon's mother turned away and continued grilling: Pssssss. Psssssss.

Api ran to get her father. She found him sitting outside his sleeping hut. He too had been watching the boy stranger. He looked at Api, then at her mother, and nodded.

So when the boy stranger stood before Api's mother, she reached for her plate of foutou, chose the biggest one, and put it in his bowl. She dipped a ladle into her pot of chicken in palm nut sauce and poured it over the foutou. Then she continued her pounding: Tue, ta. Tue, ta.

The boy stranger ate silently, then left without saying a word.

Three full moons passed. No one saw the boy stranger until the morning of the next feast day. It was a *Va*, a wedding day.

On that morning Api was playing the clapping game *N'Dé* with Kousso, Chiadon, and some other girls. It was Api's turn to be in the center of the circle. As the others clapped and sang, she was supposed to fall backward, trusting the girls to catch her and stand

her back in the circle. So Api leaned in Kousso's direction. Instead of catching her, Kousso stepped aside. Api fell to the ground: Kabak!

"Aiyeee!" she yelled. Kousso and the other girls laughed, che, che, che! They laughed so hard, they hugged their bellies. Api cried and cried, hih, hih, hih.

Then Api looked up and saw the boy stranger entering the sawa. Kousso saw him too, and called out, "Look, here HE comes again. Why DOES that skinny boy keep coming back?"

They all watched as once again the boy stranger held out his bowl to Kousso's mother. Again Kousso's mother turned away and continued stirring the sauce: Ngub. Ngub.

They watched as the boy approached Chiadon's mother. Again
Chiadon's mother turned away and continued grilling the chicken:
Pssssss. Pssssss.

So again Api ran to her father, who nodded to her mother, who
gave the stranger the biggest foutou and a ladle of sauce. Then
Api's mother resumed pounding: Tue, ta. Tue, ta. As before, the
boy ate silently and left without saying a word.

Two more full moons passed before the boy stranger reappeared. This day was another feast day, a _Gnouen,_ a celebration of someone's spirit arriving in heaven. Api was playing tag with Kousso and Chiadon. She was running very fast after Kousso and had nearly caught her, when Chiadon tripped Api: Ban!

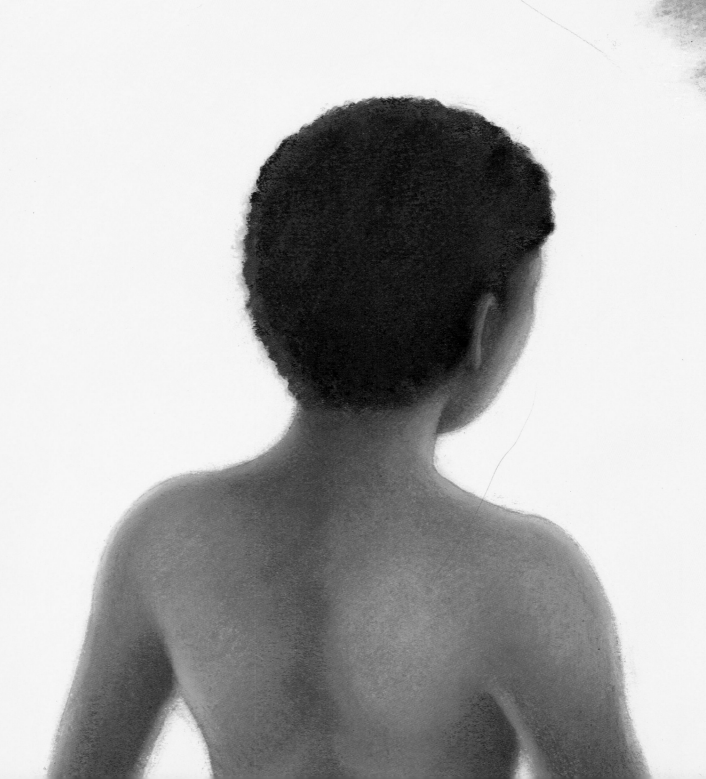

"Aiyeee!" Api yelled as she hit the ground: Kabak! Chiadon and Kousso laughed, che, che, che! Api cried and cried, hih, hih, hih. But then she looked up and once again saw the boy stranger entering the sawa.

Again the boy was turned away by Kousso's mother: Ngub. Ngub. And by Chiadon's mother: Pssssss. Pssssss. But he was fed by Api's mother, who then resumed her pounding: Tue, ta. Tue, ta. This time after the boy stranger ate, he spoke to Api's family.

"*Ahelé*," he greeted them in a low, very grown-up voice. "Kind people," he said, "on the next feast day I will not return. Instead it is you who must travel. Pack your belongings, gather your animals, and leave this village in the early morning before the cock crows. Do not stop until you have crossed the river Amman."

That said, the boy stranger left as silently as before.

One more full moon waned. On the evening before the next feast day, Api and her parents completed their packing. Then they went to say good-bye to the other villagers.

"We are leaving," said Api's mother. "The boy stranger has told us to take our belongings and walk until we have crossed the river Amman. Come with us, if you like."

"What foolishness," said Kousso's mother as she and Kousso turned away.

"Why should anyone listen to a boy beggar?" Chiadon's mother added as she and her daughter also turned away.

So Api and her parents returned to their huts and went to sleep.

They awoke before the sun, gathered their belongings and animals, and began walking across the sawa. No one else was awake. The sawa was completely quiet. But Api imagined she heard the feast-day sounds one last time:

Tue, ta. Tue, ta.

Ngub. Ngub.

Pssssss. Pssssss.

Then, just as the family reached the edge of the village, they
heard a cock crow very loudly: Ai yi yi yi yeeeee!

Api and her parents walked all day until they came to the river Amman. Then they waded across: Shush shu. Shush shu.

As they rested on the other side, their silence was suddenly shattered by a great TUE! a thousand times louder than any tue they'd heard before. And again TUE, TA! TUE, TA! TUE, TA! Wide streams of fire shot into the air above their village!

Then they heard a NGUB! a thousand times louder than any ngub they'd heard before. A great river of steaming red goo gushed from the earth of their village. Then came more goo: NGUB, NGUB. And more NGUB, NGUB, NGUB, until the village was buried and in its place stood a mountain.

Down the mountain rushed wide, steamy rivers of goo, snaking along until they reached the river Amman. Then Api and her

parents heard a PSSSSSS a thousand times louder than any pssssss they'd ever heard before. Then more PSSSSSS, PSSSSSS. And more PSSSSSS, PSSSSSS, PSSSSSS.

"Aiyeee!" Api yelled at the sight of her village being buried by the lava.

"Aiyeee! Aiyeee!" yelled her parents.

The three hugged one another and wept, hih, hih, hih.

It was late at night when Api and her parents left the river and walked a short distance to a bamboo grove. There Api's father built a fire to grill the chicken, pssssss, while Api's mother stirred the sauce, ngub, and Api pounded the foutou: Tue, ta. Tue, ta.

It was the first meal in what became a new village, a village that
to this day is always willing to share its food with strangers.

## Author's Note

In Ivory Coast, West Africa, villagers of Becedi Brignan still tell the legend on which this story is based. It is the legend of the birth of their village. They believe they are the descendants of the one kind family who heeded the warning of a stranger. The legendary mountain that rose to bury their other, selfish ancestors still stands as a reminder to villagers to be kind—especially to strangers.

To this day the mountain is considered sacred. Everyone must purify their thoughts before climbing it. Nothing—not even stones or leaves—is allowed to be taken from it. Halfway up the mountain there is a tiny water hole where prayers are said to the ancestors and an offering is made by the village priest who pours a drink on the ground.

I had been living and teaching in the city of Abidjan, Ivory Coast, for about a year when I first heard this legend. I had made a trip to Becedi Brignan, wanting to know more about life in the villages of Ivory Coast. There, I learned the village story, climbed the sacred mountain, ate a traditional meal of foutou and sauces in the bamboo grove, and took a tour of the village.

Intrigued by both the legend and the village, I decided to write a story based on the legend and to include details of present-day village life so that children who read the story might gain some insight into the lives of Ivorian village children. I returned to the village, notebook and camera in hand. For further information on the local language, food, customs, and children's games, I consulted a village elder, Abi Adjoualé. I dreamed that—should the book be published—some of the proceeds could be used to benefit the children of Becedi Brignan. That dream came true and the children now have a school cafeteria—a paillote—in which hot lunches are served.